Book of Mormon Rhymes

A Companion for Family Scripture Study

DEBBI S. ROLLO

https://www.bookofmormonrhymes.com

bomrhymes2@gmail.com

i

The rhymes in this book are a work of fiction based on
The Book of Mormon,
Another Testament of Jesus Christ,
The Church of Jesus Christ of Latter-day Saints.

Names, characters, places, and incidents, are based on those
found in *The Book of Mormon* with a fictional, creative license.
This work is not an official publication of the
Church of Jesus Christ of Latter-day Saints.
The views expressed herein are the responsibility of the author
and do not necessarily represent the position of the church.

First Edition

Book of Mormon Rhymes by Debbi S. Rollo
Published by Debbi S. Rollo Orem, UT 84057
Debbi Rollo, Orem, UT

ISBN: 978-0-578-52591-4

**Join Newsletter
And Visit Author's Website at**
http://www.bookofmormonrhymes.com

DEDICATION

To all the record keepers
in The Book of Mormon
Who lived and wrote their stories.

ACKNOWLEDGEMENTS

I want to thank my husband, Craig, for his years of support and patience while writing this book. My children for their feedback and support. Thanks to my son, Daniel, for the many hours he spent helping me edit. A special thanks to Jonathan Bellio who brought my rhymes to life with his beautiful illustrations that helped move this book forward.

HOW TO USE THIS BOOK

THIS BOOK CAN BE USED AS A COMPANION for your daily family scripture study of The Book of Mormon or simply for enjoyment. For scripture study, upon finishing a chapter or group of verses, read the rhymes for that section. I recommend reading it at least twice and take a moment to pause to share thoughts, bear testimony, and generate discussion. Rhymes are chronological with scripture references for each rhyme.

This book will reinforce and create a better understanding of the amazing stories and teachings of The Book of Mormon. It will add clarity, enlightenment, and strengthen testimonies of Jesus Christ and of The Book of Mormon. The best part – it's fun to read!

Young children will happily learn Book of Mormon stories and principles in a way they can understand and remember. Teens and adults will be delighted to discover The Book of Mormon in a new light. It is also ideal for bedtime, Come Follow Me study, family home evening, and captivating reading.

I believe with all my heart that these inspiring and carefully written rhymes will create a new love for The Book of Mormon and will bring your family closer to God.

~ Debbi S. Rollo

AUTHOR'S STORY

Shortly after the tragic death of my 23-year-old daughter and her husband, I read regularly with their two young children from a classic book of nursery rhymes. Those simple rhymes and beautiful illustrations lifted our troubled hearts and brought joy to our souls during our time of grief.

One day, while reading together, the thought came to me that there should be a book of rhymes specifically for The Book of Mormon. As I opened The Book of Mormon with this idea, rhyming words flowed into my mind. I felt as though a host of heavenly angels hovered over me, whispering the words that I should write. I felt compelled from that moment on to create this book for publication. Writing these rhymes has been one of my greatest joys.

President Ezra Taft Benson taught: "I have a vision of artists putting into film, drama, literature, music, and paintings great themes and great characters from the Book of Mormon...Indeed, I have a vision of flooding the earth with the Book of Mormon." (October 1988 General Conference, "*Flooding the Earth with the Book of Mormon*"). This book is me doing my small part to help fulfill President Benson's vision.

Table of Contents

CHAPTER THREE – *2 Nephi*
Land of Nephi

CHAPTER FOUR – *Jacob*
As A Dream

CHAPTER FIVE – *Enos-Words of Mormon*
Pass The Plates

CHAPTER SIX – *Mosiah*
Rising Generation

CHAPTER SEVEN – *Alma*
Missionary Work and War

CHAPTER EIGHT – *Helaman*
Stones and Arrows

CHAPTER NINE – *3 Nephi-4 Nephi*
Christ's Appearance

CHAPTER TEN — *Mormon*
Army Captain

CHAPTER ELEVEN – *Ether*
Jaredite Nation

CHAPTER TWELVE – *Moroni*
Moroni's Promise

Chapter One
Introduction Pages

A Marvelous Work

Title Page –
Testimony of the Prophet Joseph Smith

Rhymes 1-6

1

BOOK OF MORMON
Title Page
There was a hidden treasure,
An abridgment of God's word.
It is The Book of Mormon,
To go forth to all the world.

2

HOLY SCRIPTURES
Introduction
We have The Book of Mormon,
The Bible we have too,
Both are Holy Scriptures,
For all the world to view.

3
GOLDEN PLATES
Introduction

Moroni buried golden plates,
Sealed up carefully,
Then he appeared to Joseph Smith,
In eighteen twenty-three.

4
AN INVITATION
Introduction

I have an invitation,
Something I can do;
Read The Book of Mormon,
Then pray to know it's true.

THREE WITNESSES

Testimony of Three witnesses

David, Oliver, and Martin,
The Lord's chosen three,
Said a Heavenly Angel
Brought the plates for them to see.

Be it known unto all nations,
Kindreds, tongues and people too;
The Book of Mormon Record,
We each know it to be true.

6
ANGEL MORONI
Testimony of Prophet Joseph Smith

Angel Moroni, dressed all in white,
Awoke Joseph Smith late in the night.
Angel Moroni, while Joseph lay still,
Told of Gold Plates buried inside a hill.

CHAPTER TWO
1 NEPHI

Into The Wilderness

1 Nephi 1 – 1 Nephi 21
Rhymes 7-53

7

GOODLY PARENTS
1 Nephi 1:1

Nephi had good parents,
Good parents Nephi had.
Sariah was his Mom,
And Lehi was his Dad.

***

8

LEHI'S VISION
1 Nephi 1:18-20

Father Lehi had a vision,
A vision he did see,
Jerusalem will be destroyed,
He warned them urgently.
The people said it won't be so.
He said repent, but they said no!

9
INTO THE WILDERNESS
1 Nephi 2:2-4

Goodbye to our home,
Our silver and gold,
Sent into the wilderness,
By the Lord we're told.

Farewell to our friends,
We must now depart,
Sent into the wilderness,
For a brand-new start.

10
NEAR THE RED SEA
1 Nephi 2:5

Sit near the Red Sea, Nephi,
Next to your brother Sam.
Splash in the water, Lehi,
Where others may have swam.
Sit near the Red Sea, Laman,
By Sariah, mother dear.
Walk on the Seashore, Lemuel,
And know the Lord is near.

11
RIVER AND VALLEY
1 Nephi 2:9-10

Laman, be like this river,
Lemuel, be like this land,
In all righteousness,
Firm and steadfast stand.

12

GO AND DO
1 Nephi 3:7

I will go and do, said Nephi,
The Lord prepares a way,
To keep all His commandments,
To follow and obey.

13

PLATES OF BRASS
1 Nephi 3:9 – 4:24

Laman and his brothers went,
With gold to trade for plates.
They were told to go away,
And fled outside the gates.

Nephi crept to Laban's house,
To go obtain the plates.
Nephi took the plates of brass,
And fled outside the gates.

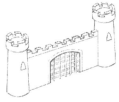

14
LET US GO UP
1 Nephi 4:1-2

Let us go up,
Let us be strong,
Let us be faithful too;
Up like Nephi,
Strong like Moses,
Faithful, good, and true.

15

ZORAM'S OATH
1 Nephi 4:30-38

Zoram, Laban's servant,
With Nephi fled away,
Then Zoram made an oath;
With Nephi he would stay.

***

16

SARIAH'S SONS
1 Nephi 5:1-7

Where are my four sons?
Are they perhaps no more?
Hooray! I hear them coming,
Outside of my tent door.

17
LEHI'S SEARCH
1 Nephi 5:10-16

Lehi searched the records,
Brought from Laban's town,
Written on the brass plates,
This is what he found:

Five Books of Moses,
About Adam and Eve,
Words of Jeremiah,
Many prophecies.
Lehi also read,
His genealogy,
Of Jacob and Joseph,
Led out of captivity.

18

IN OUR HAND

1 Nephi 5:21-22

We now have the plates,
Firmly in our hand,
On our sacred journey,
Toward the Promised Land.

***

19

THINGS OF WORTH

1 Nephi 6:5-6

What will Nephi write,
On the plates tonight?
Words that are of worth,
To children here on earth.

20
OFF THEY SKIP
1 Nephi 7:1-4

Off they march to get a wife,
Hee-De Hi-De-Ho.
Off they skip to Ishmael's house,
Lehi's sons do go.

21
NEPHI'S BROTHERS
1 Nephi 7:16-21

Nephi's brothers hit him,
And tied up both his hands.
Nephi prayed for the strength,
To burst his leather bands.
They hit him once again,
Though angels did forbid.
Nephi showed forgiveness,
For what his brothers did.

22
TREE OF LIFE
1 Nephi 8

Laman, Lemuel come along,
On the narrow path so strong.
Taste the fruit that's on the tree,
God's sweet gift for you and me.
Cling to the rod; come this way,
On the trail where we can play.
Taste the fruit that's on the tree,
God's sweet gift for you and me.

23
PLATES OF NEPHI
1 Nephi 9

Why two sets of records?
Why two sets of plates?
For the lord's wise purpose,
So First-Nephi states.

***

24
JERUSALEM
1 Nephi 10:1-14

Our great city, Jerusalem,
Will be destroyed soon;
Scattering and gathering,
Below the big, bright moon.

25

SIX HUNDRED YEARS
1 Nephi 10:4-6

If I were born six hundred years
From now, then I would see,
The Savior of the world be born,
And die to set us free.

***

26

MYSTERIES
1 Nephi 10:19

Seek, ye children, seek,
And mysteries you'll find.
Through the Holy Ghost,
They'll come into your mind.

27
NEPHI'S VISION
1 Nephi 11

Nephi knelt in humble awe,
To see all that his father saw,
A vision of the Lamb and tree,
And future things to one day be.

***

28
A PEEK
1 Nephi 12

A peek into the future,
The Lord let Nephi see,
Future wars and disbelief,
Of his posterity.

29
MAN ON THE SEA
1 Nephi 13:10-14

Look, said the angel,
At the man on the sea,
Led by the Spirit,
To fulfill prophecy.
Look at the Gentiles,
The angel did say,
In ships on the waters,
Who will come here one day!

30
UNTO THE GENTILES
1 Nephi 13:34

Unto the Gentiles,
The gospel will go,
The truth, plain and precious,
One day they will know.

31

GREAT AND MARVELOUS
1 Nephi 14:7

A great and marvelous work,
Among the children of men,
Will bring ever-lasting peace,
To the Lord's people again.

***

32

JOHN
1 Nephi 14:19-27

A man dressed in white,
Is going to write,
Many things that he will be shown.
They will be in a book,
For the people to look;
By the name of John he is known.

33

IF I

1 Nephi 15:11

If I faithfully believe,
The Lord says I'll receive.
If I harden not my heart,
The Lord will then impart.

34

THE OLIVE TREE

1 Nephi 15:13-16

Bring the branches to the hill,
Where the olive tree stands still.
Graft them near the natural twigs,
Bringing shade to all the kids.

The Gentiles will one day be,
Grafted into the olive tree.
All God's children will be told,
How to come unto His fold.

35

LIAHONA
1 Nephi 16:9-10

Lehi awoke one morning,
And found beside his tent,
A very special present,
One that the Lord had sent.
It's called the Li-a-hon-a,
A round ball made of brass.
It was sent to point the way,
To journey on their path.

36
NEPHI'S BROKEN BOW
1 Nephi 16:18-23

Yikes! Oh no,
Nephi broke his bow!
Aw, How sad,
Now his family's mad.
Hey! They booed,
How will we get food?
Look! He bade,
A new bow I made.
Hip–hooray!
Nephi saved the day!

37

NEPHI HUNTS FOR FOOD
1 Nephi 16:23-31

Where shall Nephi hunt for food,
With his wooden bow?
Directed by the brass ball,
He knows where to go.

Where did Nephi hunt for food,
With his wooden bow?
High upon the mountain-top,
He faithfully did go.

***

38

BY SMALL MEANS
1 Nephi 16:29

And thus we see,
That by small means,
The Lord can bring
About great things.

39

IN BOUNTIFUL

1 Nephi 17:4-8

Eight years in the wilderness,
On Lehi's family trip,
In Bountiful, the Lord,
Told Nephi, build a ship.

***

40

MAKING TOOLS

1 Nephi 17:9-10

Off goes Nephi to make tools,
But first he kneels to pray.
Off he goes to find some ore,
The Lord leading the way.

41

BUILD A SHIP
1 Nephi 17:16-18

Nephi wants to build a ship,
With tools he made from rock.
He thinks the Lord commanded it,
Laman and Lemuel mock.

42

DO ALL THINGS
1 Nephi 17:50-51

If God commanded me,
To do all things I could.
If God commanded me,
To do all things I would.

I could tell this water,
To turn to earth right now,
And I can build a ship;
The Lord will show me how.

43
BOARD THE SHIP
1 Nephi 18:5-6

Little children pack your bags,
Go collect some honey.
Tomorrow we go into the ship,
When it's bright and sunny.

Prepare fruit and load the seeds,
Gather up toys and meat.
It's almost time to board the ship,
And get into your seat.

44

SHIP A-SAILING
1 Nephi 18:8

There was a ship a-sailing,
On the sea so grand,
Lehi's family a-singing,
Toward the Promised Land.

45

ON THE SEA
1 Nephi 18:9-21

Ishmael's sons and Nephi's brothers,
Acted rude toward one another.
They forgot about the Lord,
And bound Nephi with a cord.
They almost drowned in the sea,
Until Nephi was set free.

46

LAND-HO
1 Nephi 18:23

Land-ho, Land-ho, Land-ho,
The Promised Land at last!
Go forth and pitch your tents,
And so it came to pass.

**

47

SEEDS
1 Nephi 18:24

In each pocket I have seeds,
To plant in fertile soil.
In the Promised Land we work,
To build, to plant and toil.

48
TREASURE HUNT
1 Nephi 18:25

Going on a treasure hunt,
Wonder what we'll find?
Some copper, gold, and silver,
Animals, all kinds.

Going on a treasure hunt,
Digging in the sand.
You never know what you'll find,
In the Promised Land.

49
DIGGING ORE
1 Nephi 19:1

Let's dig ore for Nephi,
To use to make new plates,
Then bring it to his tent,
Where Nephi sits and waits.

50

PROPHECY OF JESUS
1 Nephi 19:8-9

A prophecy of Jesus,
An Angel did proclaim,
In six hundred years from now,
He'll come and suffer pain.

***

51

PROPHETS OF OLD
1 Nephi 19:18-20

Nephi wrote these things,
To bring us to the Lord,
And saw many things,
As prophets saw of old.

52

HEARKEN AND HEAR
1 Nephi 20

Hearken and hear this,
Isaiah boldly claims;
Israel has been chosen,
In the Savior's name.

***

53

O HOUSE OF ISRAEL
1 Nephi 21

O house of Israel,
O isles of the sea,
O ye my people,
O listen to me.
O house of Israel,
O heavens, O earth,
O Gentiles, the Lord,
Knows of your great worth.

CHAPTER THREE
2 NEPHI

Land of Nephi

2 Nephi 1 – 2 Nephi 33
Rhymes 54-79

54
HAND OF THE LORD
2 Nephi 1:6

None can come to this land,
Save they shall be brought,
By the hand of the Lord,
Lehi clearly taught.

55
DEEP SLEEP
2 Nephi 1:14

Awake! Awake,
From a deep sleep,
Shake off the chains you wear.
Awake, arise
From the grave's dust,
In cold and silent air.

56

ZORAM

2 Nephi 1:30-31

Zoram and Nephi were friends,
True friends the two came to be.
Zoram was given a blessing,
By Lehi, who spoke favor'bly.

***

57

OPPOSITION

2 Nephi 2

There is good, so there is bad,
Opposition there must be.
When we choose Jesus Christ,
We're blessed for eternity.

58

LITTLE JOSEPH

2 Nephi 3:25

Little brother Joseph,
Was Lehi's last-born son.
He was blessed by Lehi,
Then ran off to have fun.

***

59

LEHI GREW OLD

2 Nephi 4:3-12

Lehi grew old,
Before he died,
His Grandchildren he did bless.
He said be good,
And keep God's laws,
Repent, and your sins confess.

60

PSALM OF NEPHI
2 Nephi 4:16-17

Nephi loves the scriptures,
He ponders and he prays,
And yet his heart cries out,
To stop his wicked ways.

61

FAITHFUL CREW
2 Nephi 5:5-6

Nephi was warned to leave;
The Lord said not to stay,
With his wicked brothers,
And so he moved away.

There goes Nephi, Jacob, Sam,
With Zoram and Joseph too.
Also Nephi's sisters,
Oh what a faithful crew!

62

LAND OF NEPHI

2 Nephi 5:7-8

What should we call the name,
Where will we pitch our tents?
Let us call it Nephi,
The people did consent.

***

63

A TEMPLE

2 Nephi 5:15-17

Building buildings,
Working wood,
We labor with our hands.
Nephi said,
We will build,
A Temple in the land.

64

NO KING

2 Nephi 5:18-19

Nephi, Nephi be our king,
The people cheered and said.
No, I will not be your king,
But will rule and teach instead.

***

65

LET US GATHER

2 Nephi 6-8

Let us gather together,
Tonight near the creek,
To hear words of Isaiah,
That Jacob will speak.

66

HEARKEN, HEARKEN
2 Nephi 8:4-11

Hearken, hearken can't you see,
The law shall proceed from me.
Awake, as in ancient day,
Sorrow shall all flee away.

***

67

PERFECT STATE
2 Nephi 9:1-13

When my body dies,
My spirit stays alive,
And because of Jesus Christ,
In heaven I'll arrive.

When my body dies,
My spirit will await,
'Til I get my body back,
In its perfect state.

68
ISAIAH'S WORDS
2 Nephi 11:1-2

Nephi saw the Savior,
And Jacob saw him too.
Nephi testified that
Isaiah's words are true.

***

69
TOP OF THE MOUNTAINS
2 Nephi 12:2-3

In the top of the mountains,
All the nations will flow,
In the last days to Zion,
Be ready to go.

70
COMPARE ISAIAH
2 Nephi 12-24

Compare Isaiah chapter two,
Through chapter twenty-four,
And read Isaiah's prophecies,
To see what lies in store.

***

71
DAUGHTERS OF ZION
2 Nephi 13:16-20

The daughters of Zion are haughty,
Walking and mincing they go.
The daughters of Zion are naughty,
Tingling feet down below.
Their fancy chains, bracelets and bonnets,
Bright headbands, earrings and jewels,
Are the things the daughters do worship,
Instead of obeying God's rules.

72

ALL HIS CHILDREN
2 Nephi 26:33

Black, white, bond and free,
Male and female too,
God loves all His children,
Both Gentile and Jew.

***

73

UPON THE HOUSETOPS
2 Nephi 27:11

Upon the housetops,
The book will be read,
It is sealed to come forth,
As Isaiah has said.

74
A BIBLE, A BIBLE
2 Nephi 29:3-10

A Bible! A Bible!
The Gentiles do say,
We need no more Bible,
So go off and play.

The Lord loves his people,
All nations on earth,
And gives us His words,
For they have great worth.

75

IN THE NORTH
2 Nephi 29:11

In the north, in the south,
And in the east and west,
The Lord commands His words,
To be made manifest.

76

WOLF AND THE LAMB
2 Nephi 30:12-13

The wolf and the lamb,
Will nap with the calf,
Along with the lion,
And children who laugh.

The cow and the bear,
Will feed near the fox,
Along with the lion,
Eats straw like the ox.

77

WHO SAID

2 Nephi 31

Who said repent and always pray,
From God to never go astray?
Who said God's laws, always obey?
Jesus taught this is the way.

***

78

FEAST UPON

2 Nephi 32:3

Feast upon the words of Christ,
And trust that they are true.
Feast upon the words of Christ,
They'll tell you what to do.

79
FAREWELL
2 Nephi 33:12-14

Goodbye and farewell,
'Til we meet at that great day.
Goodbye and farewell,
Nephi wrote, then went away.

CHAPTER FOUR
JACOB

As A Dream

Jacob 1 – Jacob 7
Rhymes 80–85

80

SECOND NEPHI

Jacob 1:9-11

Nephi was getting old,
He knew he soon would die.
He chose a king to lead,
Known as Second-Nephi.

***

81

ONE WIFE

Jacob 2

Jacob had a lot to say,
About the people's wicked way.
They should obtain a hope in Christ,
And men should only have one wife.

82

IN THE VINEYARD
Jacob 5-6

Deep in the vineyard,
An olive tree stands,
With dying branches,
In rich, fertile land.

Pluck off the branches,
That do not bear fruit,
Then burn them with fire,
Preserving the root.

83

WICKED SHEREM
Jacob 7:1-21

Oh, wicked Sherem,
He could not speak a sound.
He asked for a sign,
Then fell down to the ground.

84

AS A DREAM

Jacob 7:26

Time did pass away,
As if it were a dream,
A lonesome people,
As wanderers it seemed.
Cast out from Jerusalem,
Solemn in all our ways,
Hated of our brethren,
We mourned out all our days.

***

85

ADIEu

Jacob 7:27

Little brother, Jacob,
Oh, what did he do?
Gave the Plates to Enos,
And wrote to us, adieu.

CHAPTER FIVE
ENOS—WORDS OF MORMON

Pass The Plates

Enos 1 – Words of Mormon 1
Rhymes 86-91

86

ENOS WENT A-HUNTING

Enos 1:3-6

Enos went a-hunting,
And in the forest prayed.
He asked for forgiveness,
Through the night and day.

***

87

A MANSION

Enos 1:27

There is a place prepared for us,
To enter when we die,
A mansion where our Father dwells,
Enos testified.

88
PASS THE PLATES
Jarom 1-Omni 1:1-12

Enos passed to Jarom,
Jarom passed them on,
Passed the Plates to Omni,
Then to Am-ar-on.
Am-ar-on passed to Chemish,
Who then passed them on,
Passed down to Amal-eki,
But first Abin-a-dom.

***

89
AMALEKI
Omni 1:23-25

Amaleki, Amaleki,
Saw that he was growing old,
So he passed the records down,
To King Benjamin, we're told.

90

IN SEARCH OF NEPHI

Omni 1:27-30

A strong and a mighty man,
With others went away,
In search of the land, Nephi,
Where they wished to stay.
They returned with sorrow,
Only fifty had survived.
Off went another group;
No one knows if they arrived.

***

91

ABRIDGED

words of Mormon 1

I finish out my record,
Brave Mormon wrote one day,
Then passed it to Moroni,
Abridged in the Lord's way.

CHAPTER SIX
MOSIAH

Rising Generation

Mosiah 1 – Mosiah 29
Rhymes 92-127

92
FUTURE KING
Mosiah 1:10

Mosiah will be king,
King Benjamin said so.
Gather all the people,
To let the kingdom know.

***

93
TENTS FACING EAST
Mosiah 2:1-6

Gather near the Temple,
With tents facing East,
Look up at the tower,
King Benjamin speaks.

94
GREAT KING BENJAMIN
Mosiah 2:8-17

Oh Great King Benjamin,
Upon the tower tall,
From my tent I'll listen,
Although I'm very small.

95
AWAKE
Mosiah 3:1-17

Awake, and he awoke,
And there an angel stood,
To declare glad tidings,
A message that was good.
King Benjamin was told,
That Jesus Christ will be,
Born into the world,
To die for you and me.

96

THE PEOPLE FELL
Mosiah 4:1-2

To the ground, people fell,
All of the righteous folk.
With one voice crying out,
For mercy they invoke.

97

BELIEVE IN GOD
Mosiah 4:9-10

Believe in God,
That He is,
And created all.
Believe in God,
That He will,
Save us from the Fall.
Believe in God,
That He has,
All wisdom to impart.
Believe in God,
That He knows,
What is in our heart.

98

BORROWED

Mosiah 4:28

I'm off to my neighbor's,
To go see them again,
And return what I borrowed,
So I won't commit sin.

***

99

HOW MANY

Mosiah 6:1-2

How many people,
Did not enter the fold?
Except little children,
Not one single soul.
How many are numbered,
And how do we know?
King Benjamin counted,
A long time ago.

100

OUR NEW KING
Mosiah 6:3-4

Hail to our new king!
Mosiah rules and reigns.
Goodbye, King Benjamin,
Your message will remain.

101

SIXTEEN STRONG MEN
Mosiah 7:1-5

Sixteen strong and mighty men,
Searching for a land,
In search of Lehi-Nephi,
Treading through the sand.

Sixteen strong and mighty men,
Grateful and amazed,
Discovered Lehi-Nephi,
After forty days.

102

AMMON AND AMALEKI
Mosiah 7:6-15

Ammon and Amal-e-ki,
Went into the land, Nephi.
Into prison they were sent,
Then before the king they went.
Ammon bravely raised his voice,
Happily, the king rejoiced.
He released them from their cell,
In Zarahemla they will dwell.

***

103

KING MOSIAH CAN
Mosiah 8:8-13

Who can translate golden plates,
From a distant land?
I know, I know, cried Ammon,
King Mosiah can!

104

OVER-ZEALOUS ZENNIF
Mosiah 9:1-13

Over-zealous Zennif,
Left with a group of men.
Enslaved by the Lamanites,
They couldn't go home again.

105

ZENNIF'S SON, NOAH
Mosiah 11:1-9

Zennif's son, Noah, was king.
He reigned in wickedness.
He over-taxed his people,
A fifth-part of their ziff.

Zennif's son, Noah, was king.
He worshipped gold and stone.
He lied to all his people,
While sitting upon his throne.

106
NOAH BUILT A TOWER
Mosiah 11:12-15

Noah built a tower,
Near the temple on a hill,
To look 'round about,
From his window-sill

His heart was set on riches,
Taxation did incur,
Noah was a selfish king,
And a wine-bibber.

***

107
ABINADI'S DISGUISE
Mosiah 12:1

Abinadi wore a costume,
A mysterious disguise,
Then entered into the city,
To preach and to prophesy.

108

SMITTEN

Mosiah 13

Abinadi cried, if you touch me,
You will be smitten by God!
Then he finished his message,
About their evil and fraud.

***

109

ISIAH SAY

Mosiah 14:1-6

Yeah, doth not Isaiah say,
We, like sheep, have gone astray?
Everyone in his own way,
Even doth Isaiah say.

110

ABINADI'S LAST BREATH
Mosiah 17

Abinadi the Prophet,
Taught that Jesus will bring peace.
When the king said to kill him,
Alma plead for his release.

Abinadi the Prophet,
Burned by fire was his death.
You'll die like me, King Noah,
Was Abinadi's last breath.

***

111

ALMA BELIEVED
Mosiah 17:1-4

Alma believed Abinadi,
With great humility.
The king's servants tried to slay him,
So Alma had to flee.

112

ALMA'S HIDING PLACE
Mosiah 18:1-7

Among the birds and buzzing bees,
In a thicket of small trees,
People hear about God's grace,
In Alma's secret hiding place.

***

113

WATERS OF MORMON
Mosiah 18:8-16

How many were baptized,
By Alma near the shore?
In the Waters of Mormon,
Were two-hundred and four.

114

WICKED KING NOAH
Mosiah 19:2-20

Wicked King Noah, you better run,
Chasing right behind you is Gideon.
Wicked King Noah, too late to cry,
Should have listened to Abinadi!

***

115

LAMANITE GIRLS
Mosiah 20:1-5

While Lamanite girls sang and danced,
King Noah's priests secretly advanced.
Then they carried them away,
Where they went, no one could say.

116

THE ESCAPE
Mosiah 24:16-20

Hush, hush now, don't make a peep,
Lamanites are fast asleep.
Pack up food and gather sheep,
Quietly, tip-toe, let's sneak.

***

117

ALMA LED THE WAY
Mosiah 24:20-25

Alma led the way,
Twelve days, they arrived,
In Zarahemla,
Grateful they survived.

118

WORDS OF ZENIFF
Mosiah 25:4-7

Hear the words of Zeniff,
That King Mosiah reads,
And of Alma's journey,
About his Godly deeds.

***

119

OFF TO CHURCH
Mosiah 25:21-24

Off to church in Zarahemla,
Up the hill with glee.
Off to church in Zarahemla,
Church of God are we.

120
RISING GENERATION
Mosiah 26:1-4

The rising generation,
Chose not to believe.
The rising generation,
Satan did deceive.
The rising generation,
Let go of the iron rod.
The rising generation,
Left the Church of God.

***

121
PROCLAMATION
Mosiah 27:2-4

Hear ye, O Hear ye,
A new strict command,
From King Mosiah,
Throughout all the land.
To all the churches,
Persecution must cease,
Proclaimed the king,
To bring about peace.

122

ALMA THE YOUNGER
Mosiah 27:8-10

Alma the younger,
Was taught the Lord's way,
But chose to be wicked,
And lead others astray.

***

123

THE UNBELIEVERS
Mosiah 27:8

Uh oh, the unbelievers,
Stirring up some trouble,
Alma and Mosiah's sons,
Get out on the double!

124

ALMA SEES AN ANGEL
Mosiah 27:10-24

Alma taught against the church,
An angel did appear.
Alma and Mosiah's sons,
Were all struck down with fear.

Alma fell and couldn't get up,
As though he were dead.
I've repented of my sins,
He sat up and said.

***

125

SONS OF MOSIAH
Mosiah 27:10-35

The sons of Mosiah
Were once very bad,
But they followed the Lord,
After visions they had.

126
WHO WILL BE KING
Mosiah 28:1-10

Who will be king, asked Mosiah?
Not I, replied Ammon; Not I, Aaron said.
So did Omner and Himni;
We are going on missions instead.

***

127
CHIEF-JuDGE ALMA
Mosiah 29:41-43

Have you read the proclamation,
Declared throughout the town?
Alma will be the first Chief-Judge;
No King will wear the crown.

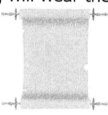

CHAPTER SEVEN
ALMA

Missionary Work and War

Alma 1 – Alma 62
Rhymes 128-173

128

NEHOR

Alma 1:2-5

Big and strong Nehor,
A wicked man was he,
Taught against God's church,
So he could get money.

***

129

KNOCK KNOCK

Alma 2:1-10

Knock, knock, who's there?
Wicked Amli-ci.
You are not our king,
So just pass us by.

Knock, knock, let me in,
I now lead this land.
I was voted king,
Of my wicked band.

130
AMLI-CITE WAR
Alma 2:11-28

The Amli-cite war rages,
Far upon the hill,
Nephites against Amli-cites,
Such a deathly chill.
Chief Captains of the armies,
Fight with stones and slings,
Armed with bows and arrows,
Such suffering war brings.

131
NEPHITE SOLDIERS
Alma 2:29-3:1

The battle has ended,
Lives have been extended,
Nephite soldiers courageously roam.
Amlici is no more,
Alma triumphed in war,
Nephite solders are now marching home.

132

THE MARK

Alma 3:4-14

A dark, round mark,
So small and red,
On the Amli-cites foreheads.
They set the mark,
God's laws denied,
As the scriptures prophesied.

***

133

WHICH SPIRIT

Alma 3:26

Which spirit, I wonder,
Will I list to obey?
A good or bad spirit,
This bright, sunny day?

134

BAPTIZED WITH CHEER

Alma 4:5

In the reign of the judges,
Of the seventh year,
Three thousand, five hundred,
Were baptized with cheer.

135

NEPI-HAH

Alma 4:7-20

Nephi-hah, Nephi-hah,
Appointed to be,
A wise judge in office,
To judge righteously.

136

ALMA PREACHES

Alma 4:20

Alma left the judgement seat,
To serve the Lord instead.
Alma preaches on the street,
To those who are misled.

137

REDEEMING LOVE
Alma 5:19-26

With pure hearts and clean hands,
Little children understand,
Heard by God up above,
Song of His Redeeming Love.

***

138

THE TREE
Alma 5:52

The tree that doesn't bring good fruit,
Shall be hewn down without dispute,
Into the fire without refute,
The ax is laid at the tree's root.

139
HUNGRY WOLVES
Alma 5:59-60

Shepherds watch for hungry wolves,
While the flocks all sleep.
Jesus is our true shepherd,
We are all His sheep.

***

140
CHURCH IN ZARAHEMLA
Alma 6:1-6

The Church in Zarahemla,
Has Priests who are ordained,
And Elders who all gather,
In sunshine, sleet and rain.

141

HIPPETY-HOP

Alma 7

Hippety-hop to Gideon,
Alma went on his way,
He is off to teach of Jesus,
And show them how to pray.

***

142

ALMA'S NEW FRIEND

Alma 7-9

Faithful and steady Alma,
Goes far away to preach.
In Gideon and Melek,
He gives a splendid speech.
Then off to Ammon-i-hah,
His words they do reject.
But then he meets an Angel,
And new friend, Amulek.

143

RATHER HAVE FUN
Alma 10:6

Have I been called many times,
Yet ignored all the signs,
As Amulek said to have done?
Do I harden my heart,
Ignoring my part,
Because I would rather have fun?

***

144

AMULEK'S JOURNEY
Alma 10:7

Amulek went on a journey,
To visit some of his kin,
Then he was stopped by an angel,
Who said to go home again.

The angel said that a Prophet,
Was hungry and needed food.
Amulek journeyed back home,
And did so with fortitude.

145

GOLD AND SILVER
Alma 11:7-19

Can I buy a measure of barley?
Yes, you can for a senine of gold.
I can pay a senum of silver,
For the worth is the same I am told.

146

AMULEK IS TEMPTED
Alma 11:21-23

Money, come get money,
Six onties of silver for you.
Amulek, open your hand,
And take the silver, so grand,
Deny God, is all you need do.

Zeezrom, do not tempt me,
To deny what I know is true.
Amulek held up his hand,
Said, it is God that is grand,
Deny Him, I never will do.

147
ZEEZROM
Alma 12-15

Zeezrom listened to Alma,
And words that Amulek spake,
Zeezrom was caught in a lie,
Guilty, he started to shake.

Zeezrom had a bad fever,
Because of sins from his past.
Zeezrom then had a blessing,
And he was healed, just like that.

Zeezrom followed the Spirit,
Humbled, he chose to believe.
Zeezrom wished to be baptized,
And was no longer deceived.

148

AMuLEK AND ALMA

Alma 15:16

Amulek had friends and fam'ly,
Who from God had turned away.
Amulek gave up his riches,
And with Alma he did stay.

***

149

FRIENDS

Alma 17:1-2

Guess who Alma spotted,
Walking to Manti?
He met Ammon, Aaron,
Omner and Himni.
Guess what they were doing,
When they met that day?
Serving faithful missions,
Going their own way.

150

OFF TO SERVE MISSIONS
Alma 17:16-19

The Sons of Mosiah,
And Ammon as well,
Went off to serve missions,
Christ's teachings to tell.

***

151

AMMON GUARDING SHEEP
Alma 17:20-39

The king's flocks were scattered,
Servants bowed down to weep,
But Ammon, with courage,
Defended the sheep.

152
THE SILENT KING
Alma 18:14

One minute,
Two minutes,
Three minutes more,
What is King Lamoni
Still waiting for?
Twenty minutes,
Thirty minutes,
Now one hour,
The silent king marvels,
At Ammon's pow'r.

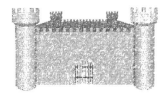

153
HE IS NOT DEAD
Alma 19:1-12

He is not dead,
He does not stink,
Cried King Lamoni's wife.
Two days in bed,
About to blink,
Lamoni's alive in Christ.

***

154
AMMON'S ON HIS WAY
Alma 20

In the land Middoni,
Aaron kneels to pray,
For release from prison,
Ammon's on his way!

155

CONVERTED LAMANITES
Alma 23:9-13

The Lamanites in Ishmael,
And those in Middoni too,
The Lamanites in Nephi,
Believed what they heard was true.
The Lamanites in Shalom,
And those in Lemuel too,
All converted to the Lord,
Believing what was true.

***

156

ONE AMALEKITE
Alma 23:14

Who was that one Amalekite,
Who converted and obeyed?
Who was that one Amalekite,
While all the others strayed?
Could I be the only one,
Would I dare stand alone,
Like that one Amalekite,
Who stood faithful on their own?

157

ANTI-NEPHI-LEHI'S
Alma 23:16-18

We, converted Lamanites,
Need a brand-new name,
One that will set us apart,
And not bring us shame.
Aaron and the King advise,
And we all agree,
The Anti-Nephi-Lehi's,
Our new name will be.

***

158

NOT ONE SOUL
Alma 24:5-16

Not one of the Lamanites,
Would take up arms to fight.
Not one soul would raise their sword,
Because their hearts were right.

159

LAND OF JERSHON

Alma 27:2-26

Off to Jershon we go,
The people of Ammon we'll be,
Protected by Nephites,
Anti-Nephi-Lehi's are we.

***

160

KORIHOR

Alma 30

Korihor, the Anti-Christ,
Claimed God did not exist.
All things prove there is a God,
He easily dismissed.
Korihor, the Anti-Christ,
Satan had led astray.
For a sign, he was struck dumb,
And in the street did lay.

161

RAMEuMPTON

Alma 31:12-23

In Ram-e-umpton,
Each Zoramite stood,
Looking towards heaven,
On a stand made of wood.
Then each Zoramite,
High upon the stand,
Spoke these self-same words,
Raising both their hands:
We do not believe in Christ,
And only we are blessed.
We thank thee we are chosen,
And know we are the best.

***

162

ALMA'S PRAYER

Alma 31:24-35

Alma, sorrowing did pray,
At the wickedness he saw,
Of the prideful Zoramites,
Who did not obey God's law.

163
THIS LIFE
Alma 34:32

Behold, this life is to repent,
Tell all your friends and neighbors.
Amulek taught that this life,
Is to perform our labors.

***

164
SONS OF ALMA
Alma 36-42

Helaman, do not be slothful,
Shiblon do not boast,
Corianton seek forgiveness;
Heed the Holy Ghost.
If you keep your faith,
Joy you will find,
Go declare God's word,
With a sober mind.

165
OUR SPIRITS
Alma 40:11

Between death and resurrection,
There's a place our Spirits go,
Back home to Heavenly Father,
Alma taught, so we might know.

***

166
LAMANITES FLEE
Alma 43:49-50

The Nephites cried out,
To God for liberty,
And in that same hour,
The Lamanites did flee.

167

TITLE OF LIBERTY
Alma 46:11-13

Captain Moroni raised the flag,
Then bowed down prayerfully,
With sacred words placed on the pole,
Title of Liberty!

168

BAND OF CHRISTIANS
Alma 46:13-22

Hurrah, the band of Christians,
They are such a sight to see,
All running toward Moroni,
Proclaiming their liberty!

Behold, the band of Christians,
Upon the rough, sandy street,
Bowing around Moroni,
Casting garments at his feet!

169
AMALICKIAH
Alma 47

Amalick-iah lied to be,
Leader over the army.
Amalick-iah became king,
Now he's married to a queen.

***

170
TIMBERS AND TOWERS
Alma 50

Helaman has the records,
Pahoran governs the land,
Moroni prepares for war,
Timbers and towers do stand.

171

KINGMEN AND FREEMEN
Alma 51:5-7

Beware, the king-men come marching,
To overthrow everything.
Alas, the free-men proclaiming,
We say, there shall be no king!

172

STRIPLING WARRIORS
Alma 56:46-56

Two-thousand stripling warriors,
To battle we did go;
Doubt not, we'd be delivered,
Our Mothers told us so.
Never fought, yet did not fear,
From doubt we did refrain.
Of all two-thousand warriors,
Not one of us were slain.

173
MORONI AND PAHORAN
Alma 60-62

Some letters are good,
Some letters are bad.
Moroni wrote to Pahoran,
Because he was mad.
Sometimes we're wrong,
And sometimes we're right.
Moroni joined Pahoran
In battle to fight.

CHAPTER EIGHT
HELAMAN

Stones and Arrows

Helaman 1 – Helaman 16
Rhymes 174-187

174

PAHORAN

Helaman 1

Pahoran was killed by Kishkumen,
Sent by a secret band.
Pacumeni became the leader,
Of the divided land.

***

175

LITTLE NEPHITES

Helaman 3:1-14

Little Nephite footprints,
Along the dusty trail,
Toward the land northward,
Where they soon will dwell.
Little Nephites playing,
In houses of cement,
Near crowded buildings,
Where their time was spent.

176

NEPHI AND LEHI

Helaman 3:20-21

Helaman had two sons,
They were his only ones.
The oldest was Nephi,
The youngest was Lehi.

***

177

TO PREACH

Helaman 5:4

Nephi was the Chief-Judge,
But then he went away,
With his brother, Lehi,
To preach from day to day.

178
ENIRCLED BY FIRE
Helaman 5:20-50

Both captured by guards,
Cast in prison to die,
Encircled by fire,
Were Lehi and Nephi.

Their hearts took courage,
While within the hot flames,
Safe and protected,
By the angels who came.

A voice from prison,
Watching, frozen with fear,
Three hundred people,
A mild whisper did hear.

179
RICH AND WICKED
Helaman 6:11-17

The Nephites and Lamanites,
Had a lot of gold,
Lots of cloth and animals,
That they bought and sold.
The richer they became,
The worse they got along,
Then became more wicked,
While choosing to do wrong.

***

180
ROBBERS
Helaman 6:18

Kishkumen was cunning,
Gadianton was greedy,
They both became robbers,
With a secret, dark treaty.

181

NEPHI'S GARDEN
Helaman 7:9-22

Out in Nephi's garden,
On his wooden tower,
Nephi kneels in prayer,
To the Lord in sorrow.

Out in Nephi's Garden,
The word of God is sent,
By Nephi to the people,
Calling out repent.

182

POWER TO RECEIVE
Helaman 10:2-5

Nephi is blessed,
In word and deed,
What he asks God,
He will receive.

183
GREAT FAMINE
Helaman 11:2-17

God sent a great famine,
Robbers went away.
The people were humbled,
And knelt down to pray.

***

184
BACK TO ZARAHEMLA
Helaman 13:1-6

Samuel preached, but was cast out,
So he went on his way.
The voice of the Lord he heard,
Instructing him to stay.
Go back to Zarahemla,
To prophesy once more.
Warn the wicked people,
Destruction lies in store.

185

SAMUEL'S PROPHECY

Helaman 14:1-8

Behold Samuel's prophesy,
That there will be no night.
When the Son of God is born,
The heavens will shine bright.

Behold Samuel's prophesy,
A new star will arise,
One as we have never seen,
A wonder in the skies.

186

IN FIVE YEARS

Helaman 14:2

In five years from now,
When I'm big and tall,
Jesus will be born,
To come save us all.

187
SAMuEL ON THE WALL
Helaman 16:1-7

Stones and arrows in the air,
Duck your head they're everywhere,
Aimed at Samuel standing tall,
Bravely preaching on the wall.

CHAPTER NINE
3 NEPHI – 4 NEPHI

Christ's Appearance

3 Nephi – 4 Nephi
Rhymes 188-227

188

NEPHI, NEPHI

3 Nephi 1:2

Nephi, Nephi, where'd you go?
You're nowhere to be found.
You departed secretly,
Without a peep or sound.

***

189

KEEP CLOSE WATCH

3 Nephi 1:8

Keep close watch, and soon you'll see,
Signs of Samuel's prophecy,
The day when there is no night,
When the world is filled with light.
Keep close watch, and soon you'll see,
Fulfillment of his prophecy.

190

ON THIS NIGHT
3 Nephi 1:13-14

Lift up your head,
Be of good cheer,
Behold the sky,
The time is near.
On this night the sign will come,
The birth of God's first-born Son.

191

NEW STAR
3 Nephi 1:19-21

We stayed awake all night,
And saw the sky shine bright.
We noticed way up high,
The new star in the sky.
We testified it meant,
That Jesus had been sent.

192

BRAVE LACHONEUS
3 Nephi 3:1-12

Give us all your cities,
The robber did demand,
Or we'll come against you,
And take away your land.
Lachoneus was brave,
He told the robber no.
They prepared for battle,
To fight against their foe.

193

NEPHITE ARMY

3 Nephi 4:30-33

Nephite army won the war,
Gid-di-anhi leads no more.
Nephites humbly rejoice,
Giving thanks with one voice.

***

194

NOT ONE DOUBTED

3 Nephi 5:1-2

How many Nephites doubted,
About the Savior's birth?
Not one living soul did doubt,
That He had come to earth.

195

PLACE TO PLACE
3 Nephi 6:7-8

There was a city road,
That went from place to place,
And stretched from land to land,
Where little children raced.

196

KING JACOB
3 Nephi 7:9-10

Some did not believe,
In Jesus Christ, the Lord,
Like new King Jacob,
With his bright, shiny sword.

197

ALL THE TOWN
3 Nephi 8:3

All the town is talking,
Of Samuel's prophecy,
Soon three days of darkness,
Throughout the land we'll see.

198
CRUCIFIED
3 Nephi 8:6-19

The earth shook with thunder,
Dividing asunder.
The storm caused the land to change,
And the roads to rearrange.
Zarahemla was on fire,
Low mountains became higher.
Cities sunk; buildings did shake,
From the earths strong, mighty quake.
Three hours, the storm did cease,
Then the earth again knew peace.
Fulfilled as Samuel prophesied,
Jesus Christ was crucified.

199
THREE WHOLE DAYS
3 Nephi 8:20-23

My candle won't light,
Neither will my torch.
The air's pitch black,
On our front porch.

My eyes can't see,
Through the eerie haze.
It stayed like this
For three whole days.

***

200
GREAT AND TERRIBLE DAY
3 Nephi 8:24-25

The people did cry out,
With howling words to say,
Oh, had we repented,
Before this terrible day.

201

HEAVENLY VOICE

3 Nephi 9-10

Throughout all the land was heard,
The voice of God's Son,
Extending arms of mercy,
Out to everyone.

Silence and great astonishment,
People gathered in deep thought;
How oft would I have gathered you?
As a hen, but ye would not.

202

ROUND ABOUT

3 Nephi 11:1-4

'Round about the temple,
In Bountiful were we,
Talking about Jesus,
And then suddenly,
'Round about the temple,
Gathered 'round the land,
We heard words from heaven,
We did not understand.

203
CHRIST'S APPEARANCE
3 Nephi 11:5-10

Looking up toward heaven,
Oh what did people see?
A man in a white robe,
Descending perfectly.
Thought it was an angel,
But He testified,
That He was Jesus Christ,
As was prophesied.

204
ONE BY ONE
3 Nephi 11:12-15

One by one, not two by two,
Not even groups of five,
Jesus let them feel His prints,
To show He was alive.

One by one, they felt His hands,
His side and then His feet.
One by one, they all took turns,
Along the crowded street.

***

205
POWER TO BAPTIZE
3 Nephi 11:18-23

The first gift Jesus gave,
A wonderful surprise,
To Nephi and the Twelve,
Was power to baptize.

206

OLD THINGS

3 Nephi 12:47-48

Old things, taught Jesus,
Are now done away.
Now that I'm here,
Do as I say.

***

207

WHEN YOU PRAY

3 Nephi 13:1-5

Nobody likes a show-off,
Pride is not okay.
Remember to be humble,
When you stand to pray.

208
THE BEAM
3 Nephi 14:3-5

Jesus taught a parable,
To teach what we should do,
Do not put down others,
First look inside of you.

***

209
OTHER SHEEP
3 Nephi 15:17

Other sheep, not of this fold,
They will hear my voice.
There will be but one shepherd,
Gathered to rejoice.

210
BRING THE SICK
3 Nephi 17:7-8

Bring the sick,
Bring the blind,
Bring the deaf and lame.
Bring the lepers,
Bring the withered,
Bring the dumb and maimed.
Bring all the afflicted,
Faithful in God's Son,
So Jesus can heal them,
Each and every one.

211

THE BREAD

3 Nephi 18:1-3

Bring the bread,
Brake the bread,
Be reverent in your seat.
Bless the bread,
Pass the bread,
For the multitude to eat.

***

212

JESUS WILL ARRIVE

3 Nephi 19:2-3

Hustle, bustle through the night,
Labor to prepare.
Jesus will arrive tomorrow,
And I must be there.

213
TWELVE NEPHITES
3 Nephi 19:4

Jesus chose disciples,
Twelve Nephites we are told,
Ordained to find and gather,
His sheep unto the fold.

Both Timothy and Nephi,
Answered the Lord's call.
Jonas and Math-on-i-ha,
Stood up firm and tall.

Ku-man and Math-oni,
Zed-e-kiah by their side,
Sat by Jeremiah,
Their new calling to abide.

214

ISAIAH'S WORDS
3 Nephi 23:1

Search Isaiah's words,
It can be fun to do.
Search Isaiah's words,
As Jesus taught us to.

***

215

TURN THE HEART
3 Nephi 25:5-6

Elijah the Prophet,
Jesus promised to send,
To turn the heart of the fathers,
To the children again.

216

BABES SPEAK

3 Nephi 26:16

The people heard the children speak,
Even small babes, so mild and meek,
Angelic words heard through the town,
Too sacred to be written down.

217

CHRIST'S CHURCH

3 Nephi 27:3-7

Call it this,
No, call it that,
Why can't we just agree?
Tell us Lord, the name you want,
Your church on earth to be.
Don't call it this,
Don't call it that,
Christ said with clarity,
The title of my church, of course,
Should be named after me.

218

NO UNCLEAN THING
3 Nephi 27:19

No unclean thing can enter,
In the Heavens up above.
Jesus taught we must repent,
And rely upon His love.

219

KNOCK AND RECEIVE
3 Nephi 27:29

I knock upon the door,
And it will open wide,
I will be invited,
To take a step inside.

Prayer is like knocking,
On The Lord's front door,
It will be opened,
To you ever more.

220

STRAIT GATE
3 Nephi 27:33

Enter in at the strait gate,
As Jesus taught us to.
Walk along the narrow path,
And come join with the few.

221

DISCIPLE'S WISHES
3 Nephi 28:1-7

What does each disciple,
Wish they could receive,
By the Savior, Jesus Christ,
After He will leave?

Nine of Christ's disciples,
Asked on earth to stay,
Then come to His kingdom,
When they're old and gray.
The other three disciples,
Asked on earth to stay,
Until the Second Coming,
Alive until that day.

222

THREE NEPHITES
3 Nephi 28:4-9

The three Nephite disciples,
Will have no death or pain,
They will have grand adventures,
'Til Jesus comes again.

***

223

WO UNTO THOSE
3 Nephi 29:5-9

Wo unto those who do say,
Miracles have gone away.
Wo unto those who do boast,
That there is no Holy Ghost.
Wo unto those who do feel,
That God's power isn't real.
Wo unto those who deny,
Christ of whom we testify.

224

ALL THINGS IN COMMON

4 Nephi 1:2-3

No fighting, battles,
Contention or war,
All things in common,
No rich or no poor.

***

225

MIACLES

4 Nephi 1-5

Miracles are happening,
Throughout all the land,
By Jesus' disciples,
By God's mighty hand.
The sick are healed, the lame now walk,
The blind receive their sight.
The deaf can hear, the dead are raised,
All in the name of Christ.

226

ZARAHEMLA

4 Nephi 1:8

The city, Zarahemla,
Was burned by wicked men;
The Nephites and Lamanites,
Built it back up again.

227

PLAY MERRILY

4 Nephi 1:15-18

No robbers, no murders,
Envyings or strifes,
No lyings, confusion,
Or manner of –ites.
We all live together,
And play merrily,
We are prospered and blessed,
Peaceful as can be.

228
AMMARON
4 Nephi 1:48-49

Ammaron listened,
To the Spirit say,
Hide up the records,
To come forth one day.

CHAPTER TEN
MORMON

Army Captain

Mormon 1 – Mormon 9
Rhymes 229-238

148

229
MORMON WAS TEN
Mormon 1:1-4

Mormon was ten,
He listened when,
Ammaron said to him,
Go to the hill Shim.
Go search and explore,
When you're twenty-four,
For the hidden plates,
Outside city gates.
Write all you observe,
On plates to preserve.

***

230
YOUNG ARMY CAPTAIN
Mormon 2:1-2

Is the army captain,
As young as we are told?
Oh yes, Mormon is,
Just fifteen years-old.

231

LITTLE MORMON
Mormon 2

Little Mormon,
Grew up to be,
The Leader of,
A huge army.

***

232

ARMY CHIEF
Mormon 3:11

Mormon was the army chief;
His soldiers wouldn't repent,
So he refused to lead them,
Then crawled inside his tent.

233

MORMON'S PURPOSE
Mormon 3:20-22

Mormon discovered,
His purpose on earth,
To persuade others,
Their souls are of worth.

Repent, he proclaimed,
Prepare ye to meet,
Our Lord and Savior,
At the judgement-seat.

***

234

MORMON'S BATTLE CRY
Mormon 6:16-19

Sad Army Captain Mormon,
He watched his people die.
From the distant hills we hear,
His lonely battle cry.

235
WHERE WILL I GO
Mormon 8:4

Where will I go,
What will I do,
Moroni trudged along?
Oh, it matters not,
He whistled this sad song.

Where will I go,
What will I do,
Alone wrapped in a coat?
Oh, it matters not,
Moroni watched and wrote.

***

236
NO MORE NEPHITES
Mormon 8:7-10

No more Nephites anywhere,
Just Lamanites who fight.
They do not know about God,
Nor will they choose the right.

237

THREE VISITORS
Mormon 8:10-11

Remember the three Nephites,
Who tarried in the land?
To Mormon and Moroni,
They visited first-hand.

***

238

THESE STORIES
Mormon 8:14-16

One day, out of darkness,
These stories will be told.
By God's pow'r, in due time,
The gospel will unfold.

239
THE SAME
Mormon 9:9

Yesterday, today, and forever,
God remains the same.
Yesterday, today, and forever,
Moroni did proclaim.

CHAPTER ELEVEN
ETHER

Jaredite Nation

Ether 1 – Ether 15
Rhymes 240-290

240
JAREDITE RECORD
Ether 1:1-2

Come and see the hidden treasure,
Sealed up safe and sound,
A record of the Jaredites,
Limhi's people found.

***

241
RECORD KEEPER
Ether 1:6

Coriantor had a son,
Coriantor named him Ether.
He wrote about the Jaredites,
He was a record keeper.

242
FROM THE TOWER
Ether 1:33

There was a great tower,
Built in a crowded town,
All the languages changed,
People scattered around.

The family of Jared,
All ran for their lives,
Away from the tower,
With children and wives.

243

BROTHER OF JARED
Ether 1:34

Brother of Jared,
Large and strong was he;
Favored of the Lord,
He prayed mightily.

***

244

GO INQUIRE
Ether 1:34-42

Go inquire of the Lord,
Brother of Jared, so,
Our language will not be changed,
And ask where we should go.

Gather flocks of every kind,
Friends and family,
Go to the valley northward,
Where I will meet thee.

245

VALLEY NIMROD

Ether 2:1-5

Into the valley, Nimrod,
Forward through tall pines,
We carry swarms of bees,
And seeds of every kind.

Into the valley, Nimrod,
The Lord is in a cloud,
Instructing all our people,
And guiding us aloud.

246
MORI-AN-CUMER
Ether 2:13-14

Zero, One, two, three, and four,
Years in Mori-an-cumer.
Near the seashore we were sent,
Near the sea to pitch our tents.
Five years, six years, seven, eight,
In a cloud the Lord awaits.

***

247
BUILD A BARGE
Ether 2:16-21

Go to work and build a barge,
Make it small, not big and large,
Like a dish with sides so tight,
Build them to be small and light.
Make a hole to put on top,
And the bottom to unstop,
To bring air while on the sea,
The Lord directed carefully.

248

BARGES WITHOUT LIGHT
Ether 2:22-25

How will we cross great waters,
In barges without light?
Asked the Brother of Jared,
To the Lord one night.

***

249

SIXTEEN STONES
Ether 3:1-5

The brother of Jared hiked,
Swiftly down Mount Shelem,
With sixteen stones in hand,
He happ'ly carried them.
He prayed and asked the Lord,
With faith on bended knee,
To touch the stones to shine,
For when they cross the sea.

250

FINGER OF THE LORD
Ether 3:6-8

The brother of Jared fell down,
Afraid, into the mud,
Saw the finger of the Lord,
It looked like flesh and blood.

The brother of Jared saw,
The Lord stretch forth his hand,
Touch the stones, one by one,
For light when they leave land.

251

ALL ABOARD
Ether 6:4

All aboard the barges,
Bring water, food, and flocks.
Step into the vessels,
And bring your lighted rocks.

252
UPON THE WAVES
Ether 6:5-8

Tossed high upon the waves we go,
Directed where the wind will blow,
Back and forth, then up and down,
Watchful, so we will not drown.
Tossed upon the waves we flow,
Toward the Promised Land we go.

253
MONSTERS AND WHALES
Ether 6:10

Ugly monsters of the sea,
You can try, but can't catch me,
And giant whales, we're glad to know,
That you're our friend and not our foe.

254

HOORAY
Ether 6:11-12

Three hundred forty-four days,
In the water, upon the waves.
Little girls and little boys,
Having fun and making noise,
Singing praises all day long,
To the Lord in reverent song,
Happy now to play in sand,
Hooray, we've reached the Promised Land!

255

JARED AND HIS BROTHER
Ether 6:19

Jared and his brother,
Were growing old and gray.
They numbered all their people,
Before they both passed away.

256

KING ORIHAH
Ether 6:27

Make way for the dashing king,
Strutting proud and tall,
Beloved son of Jared,
Great King Orihah.

***

257

GIRLS AND LADS
Ether 7:1-2

Thirty-one sons and daughters,
King Orihah had,
Eight of his children were girls,
Twenty-three were lads.

258

WICKED CORIHOR
Ether 7:4-5

Wicked, young Prince Corihor,
Rebelled and rode away,
To gather up an army,
That he had led astray.

Wicked, young Prince Corihor,
Brought his army back home,
Put Kib in captivity,
And took his father's throne.

259

SHULE WENT UP A HILL
Ether 7:8-9

Kib's son, Shule, went up a steep hill,
To molten swords made out of steel,
To battle brother, Corihor,
His father's kingdom to restore.

260
JARED'S BROTHERS
Ether 8:1-7

King Omer's son, Jared,
A wicked son was he;
Jared put his father,
Into captivity.

Jared's younger brothers,
Saw Omer's plight was grim;
They fought him in battle,
To make him king again.

261
DAUGHTER OF JARED
Ether 8:7-12

Daughter of Jared,
Did a dance
And before Akish,
She did prance.
Her Father wanted,
To be the king;
Together they planned,
A wicked thing.

262

THE FOUNTAIN

Ether 8:26

In the fountain let us all play,
That evil may be done away,
The fountain of all righteousness,
By doing good and being blessed.

***

263

AKISH

Ether 9:1-6

Akish became a wicked man,
Who formed a secret, wicked band.
He helped Jared take the thrown,
Then by lies, made it his own.
Jared is the king no more,
Akish is king instead.
Off again to wage a war,
Creating more bloodshed.

264
AKISH'S KINGDOM
Ether 9:12

Battle after battle,
Destruction was their plight.
In Akish's kingdom,
Is thirty left to fight.

***

265
OMER AND EMER
Ether 9:13-14

Omer was King again,
He grew old and said,
Bring me my son, Emer,
To anoint in my stead.

266
FLuFFY SHEEP
Ether 9:17-20

We have cattle, cows, and goats,
And white, soft fluffy sheep.
We have swine and elephants,
And oxen that we keep.

See the silver and the gold,
Come feel my silky dress.
We have ripe fruit and fine cloth,
Oh how we have been blessed.

267
NOBLE KING EMER
Ether 9:22

Emer was a noble king,
So the scriptures say;
Saw the Son of Righteousness,
Before he passed away.

268
A GREAT DEARTH
Ether 9:28-30

Serpents that are poisonous,
No rain upon the earth,
Because of our wickedness,
Came this great, ghastly dearth.

269
PITTER PATTER
Ether 9:35

Pitter Patter all around,
Rain is falling to the ground.
In Muddy puddles we all play,
Yippee, the famine's gone away!

270

RIPLAKISH

Ether 10:5-8

Riplakish, the lazy king,
Sat on his throne of gold.
His people paid high taxes,
And did as they were told.

Riplakish, the lazy king,
His people did rebel.
The king was slain in battle,
And so his kingdom fell.

***

271

LIB THE GREAT HUNTER

Ether 10:19-20

Lib, the great hunter,
Built a great big city, so grand,
In a narrow place,
Where the sea divides the land.

272

UP HILL

Ether 10:22-26

Trading silver, iron and gold,
Brass and copper, bought and sold.
We have tools to plow up hill,
To dig, explore, work and till.

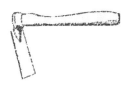

***

273

DAYS OF COM

Ether 10:33

In the days of Com the King,
Robbers crept through town,
With their wicked plans of old,
To bring the Kingdom down.

274
THE PROPHETS
Ether 11:2

Make way for the Prophets,
Coming forth to preach.
Boo, yelled all the people,
We reject your speech.

275
SHIBLOM'S BROTHER
Ether 11:5-8

Shiblom had a brother,
People should avoid,
Who said God's believers,
Should all be destroyed.
Because of iniquity,
Wars and famines came,
'Til the wicked would repent,
Pestilence remained.

276

PROPHET ETHER
Ether 12:2-4

Hope for a better world,
Is fulfilled through faith.
Let us all be steadfast,
As Prophet Ether saith.

***

277

FAITH
Ether 12:6

Faith is what you hope for,
But what you cannot see.
You'll receive a witness,
As you live faithfully.

278
WEAK THINGS
Ether 12:27

I'll come unto the Savior,
Faithfully along.
When I choose humility,
Weak things become strong.

***

279
FACE TO FACE
Ether 12:39-41

Jesus talked to Moroni,
He spoke with him face to face.
Jesus spoke to Moroni,
About charity and grace.

280
THE NEW JERUSALEM
Ether 13:6-9

In the New Jerusalem,
Children will run and play,
Built up in America,
When old things pass away.

A new heaven, a new earth,
Through Christ it will unfold,
Built up in America,
Like Jerusalem of old.

281
FIRST WILL BE LAST
Ether 13:11-12

Those who were first, will be last,
The last will be first,
To Jerusalem of old,
Gathered here on earth.

282
ETHER'S CAVE
Ether 13:13-15

Ether hides inside a cave,
While the day is bright,
Then he sneaks out to observe,
In the dark of night.

***

283
ETHER'S PROHECY
Ether 13:20-21

Cori-ant-umr, one day will see,
The truth of Ether's prophecy.
He must repent, or he will find,
Himself alone and left behind.

284
RUN, ETHER, RUN
Ether 13:22

Run, Ether, run,
Great danger lies in store.
Hide, Ether, hide,
From Cori-ant-umr.

***

285
BATTLE FOR THE THRONE
Ether 13:23-30

Cori-ant-umr battled,
Shar-ed for the throne.
Shar-ed won the battle,
And kingdom for his own.

Cori-ant-umr battled,
Shar-ed once again.
Shar-ed lost the battle,
Over pride and sin.

286
GREAT CURSE
Ether 14:1-2

Where are my tools and sword?
Not where I had them stored.
Other things are also gone,
Such a strange phenom-enon.
No one seems to understand,
This great curse upon the land.

***

287
LIB IS SLAIN
Ether 14:10-16

Here comes Lib, so big and tall,
Strongest soldier of them all,
Battles Cori-ant-umr,
Near the borders on the shore.
Lib pursues him, but in vain,
For in Agosh, Lib is slain.

288
ARMY OF SHIZ
Ether 14:18-31

Who is brave enough to stand,
Before the army Shiz?
Cries went out throughout the land,
Because of the carnage.
Shiz and Cori-ant-umr,
Fought unto bloodshed.
Cori-ant-umr did faint,
As though he were dead.

289
JAREDITE NATION
Ether 15:19

The Jaredite nation is falling apart,
The Lord is with them no more.
The Jaredite nation has hardened their hearts,
Destruction now lies in store.

290
FINAL BATTLE
Ether 15:28-32

In the dark, final battle,
Only two survived;
Cor-ian-tumr and Shiz,
Were still left alive.

Ether wept in sorrow,
After both had died,
Then finished his record,
That he soon would hide.

291
ETHER'S LAST WORDS
Ether 15:34

Will I be translated,
Or stay here to die?
I care not, wrote Ether,
With faith, he did cry.

What matters, wrote Ether,
Is to see God again,
To enter His kingdom,
And to be saved; Amen.

CHAPTER TWELVE
MORONI

Moroni's Promise

Moroni 1 – Moroni 10
Rhymes 292-307

292

MORONI'S PEN

Moroni 1:1-4

Moroni put away his pen,
Abridgment had come to an end,
But then he got it out again,
To write more 'til his life would end.

***

293

HOLY GHOST

Moroni 2:1-2

To his disciples, Jesus spoke,
Called each by name and said,
Ye shall receive the Holy Ghost,
With hands laid on their heads.

294

ORDAINED

Moroni 3:1-4

Priests and Teachers,
Enter this way,
To be ordained,
This happy day.

***

295

SACRAMENT BREAD

Moroni 4:1-3

Priests and Elders all knelt down,
With their face bowed to the ground,
To bless and sanctify the bread,
And listen while the prayer is said.

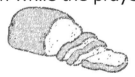

296
BAPTISM
Moroni 6:1-3
The choice to be baptized,
With a pure, broken heart,
Shows I follow Jesus,
And gives me a fresh start.

***

297
REPENT
Moroni 6:8
When I make bad choices,
Then I must repent,
Seeking for forgiveness,
Pray with real intent.

298
GOOD DEEDS
Moroni 7:5-6

Mormon preached inside a church,
He said to do good deeds,
Offer gifts with real intent,
To help all those in need.

299

SKIP TO THE FOUNTAIN
Moroni 7:10-15

Let us skip to the fountain,
To drink in the woods.
If the water tastes bitter,
The fountain's not good.

All good comes from Christ,
The devil brings sin.
I feel the difference,
From God's light within.

300
YOU WILL RECEIVE
Moroni 7:26

Ask Heavenly Father,
And if you believe,
If it is a good thing,
Then you will receive.

***

301
FAITH AND HOPE
Moroni 7:40-44

Through hope, we find our faith,
With faith, we find our way.
To live with charity,
Takes practice every day.

302

LITTLE CHLDREN
Moroni 8:5-9

Do not baptize little children,
Jesus taught us so.
Baptism for each child of God,
Is for when they grow.

***

303

BRUTAL WAR
Moroni 9:1-19

Nephites and Lamanites,
Fight a brutal war.
Mormon writes Moroni,
Of the blood and gore.
Wo unto this people,
Mormon's heart cries out,
Such wickedness and sin,
Is spreading all about.

304
ASK GOD
Moroni 10:4

When you receive these scriptures,
Then ask God if they are true.
Have faith that the Holy Ghost,
Will reveal the truth to you.

305
GIFTS OF GOD
Moroni 10:8-17

The gifts of God are many,
We each have different ones,
Given to all God's daughters,
And to His precious sons.

To teach with words of wisdom,
Or prophesy all things,
Working mighty miracles,
Of which great faith can bring.

Some have the gift of knowledge,
Of healing, and of tongues,
The gift to behold angels,
We each have different ones.

306
COME UNTO CHRIST
Moroni 10:30

Come unto Christ,
And evil resist.
Touch not the bad,
Choose every good gift.

***

307
MORONI'S FAREWELL
Moroni 10:34

Unto all, I bid farewell,
I soon go to my rest,
In the paradise of God,
After my earthly test.

Unto all, I bid farewell,
Until we reunite,
At the pleasing bar of God,
I bid you all goodnight.

THE END

Visit Website at
https://www.bookofmormonrhymes.com

Contact Debbi at
bomrhymes2@gmail.com

Sign-Up for her Newsletter and read more at
https://www.bookofmormonrhymes.com

PLEASE LEAVE AN HONEST REVIEW ON AMAZON!

Made in the USA
Las Vegas, NV
01 August 2021

27368307R00118